Charles Barney Cory

The Beautiful and Curious Birds of the World

Charles Barney Cory

The Beautiful and Curious Birds of the World

ISBN/EAN: 9783337335649

Printed in Europe, USA, Canada, Australia, Japan

Cover: Foto ©Andreas Hilbeck / pixelio.de

More available books at **www.hansebooks.com**

THE

BEAUTIFUL AND CURIOUS

BIRDS OF THE WORLD.

BY

CHARLES B. CORY,

FELLOW OF THE LINNEAN SOCIETY LONDON; FELLOW OF THE ZOÖLOGICAL SOCIETY OF LONDON; MEMBER OF THE BRITISH ORNITHOLOGISTS'
UNION, OF THE ZOÖLOGICAL SOCY OF FRANCE, OF THE NATIONAL SOCIETY OF ACCLIMATION OF FRANCE, OF THE AMERICAN ORNI-
THOLOGISTS' UNION, OF THE BOSTON SOCIETY OF NATURAL HISTORY, OF THE AMERICAN METROLOGICAL SOCIETY, OF THE
NUTTALL ORNITHOLOG. CLUB, CORRESPONDING MEMBER OF THE NEW YORK ACADEMY OF SCIENCES, ETC., ETC.
AUTHOR OF "BIRDS OF THE BAHAMA ISLANDS," ETC.

BOSTON, U. S. A.

1883.

Published by the Author for the subscribers.

PREFACE.

In writing the prent work I have striven to bring together some of the wonderful examples of the ornithological woд, and to illustrate them in such a manner that others besides naturalists may become acquainted цh the beautiful forms of bird life which inhabit our globe.

As the object of he work is so fully explained by the title, I feel that extended prefatory remarks are unnecessary, ad it only remains for me to express my thanks to my naturalist friends and to my subscribers foheir kind assistance and support.

TO

JOEL ASAPH ALLEN,

WHOSE HIGH ATTAINMENTS AS A NATURALIST

ARE SO WELL KNOWN TO ALL.

𝕿𝖍𝖎𝖘 𝖁𝖔𝖑𝖚𝖒𝖊 𝖎𝖘 𝕯𝖊𝖉𝖎𝖈𝖆𝖙𝖊𝖉,

BY HIS FRIEND,

THE AUTHOR.

LIST OF PLATES.

DIDUS INEPTUS.

DIDUS INEPTUS. *Linn.*

DODO.

IT is now nearly two centuries since a living specimen of this strange production of nature has been seen; and the only proofs which scientists have, beyond the records of history, of its having existed, are a few fragmentary remains contained in some of the European museums, the most perfect of which is a head preserved in the Ashmolean Museum at Oxford.

However, there is no doubt that at one time this huge, unwieldy species inhabited the islands of Mauritius and Bourbon, and was still abundant there as late as 1681, when the island was visited by one Benj. Harry. This record, according to Mr. H. E. Strickland ("Dodo Solitaire," etc., p. 26), is contained in the British Museum (Sloane MSS., 3668 Plut. cxi. F), and is entitled "A Coppey of Mr. Benj. Harry's Journal when he was chief mate of the Shippe Berekley Castle, Capen. Wm. Talbot then commander, on a voyage to the Coste and Bay 1679 which voyage they wintered at the Maurrisshes."

He says, "The journal is little more than a ship's log, containing many rough observations, perhaps valuable, of a brilliant comet. They left Deptford 19th November, 1679, and on their return from India, being unable to weather the Cape of Good Hope, they determined to make for 'the Marushes' the 4th of June, 1681. They saw land on the 3d of July, and on the 11th they began to build huts; and they had much labor in spreading their cargo out to dry."

"After all these turmoyles and various accidents we the beginning 7 ber brought all to a period: one parte of our misery was that that time we designed for recreation we were forc't to impt. in Labour. The ayre whilst we have been here hath been very temperate neither over hott nor over cold; itt hath been showery 3 or 4 Days sucksessively, and showery in the night sometimes a Sea Brees little wind morning and evenings.

"Now having a little respitt I will make a little description of the Island, first of its Products then of itts parts: ffirst of winged and feathered ffowle the less passant, are *Dodos whose ffiesh is very hard*, a small sort of Gees, reasonably good Teele, Curleves, Pasen ffiamingos, Turtle Doves, large Batts, many small Birdes which are good.

"The Dutch plending a propriety to the Island because of their settlement have made us pay for gontes 1d per pound or 1/2 piece of 8 per head, the which gontes are butt reasonably good, these wild, as allso the Deer which are as large as I believe any in the world, and as good ffiesh in their seasons; for these 3 pie. of 8 per head. Bullocks large 6 pie. of 8 per head; [that] ys for victualling, heer are many wild hoggs and land turtle which are very good, other small creators on the Land, as Scorpions and Musketoes, these in small numbers, Ratts and ffeys a multitude. Munkeys of various sorts.

"In the woodes Eaboney, Box, Iron wood blacke and read, a false but not lasting fire, various sortes of other wood, though heavy yett good for fiering.

"In ye Sea and River, green tortoise very good, Shirkes, Dogges, Mulletts, Jaekabeirs (butt nott good though some 70 lb), Breams, Pomfletts, Plaise, a ffishe like a Salmund, and heer soe called but full of small ffish forked, severall sortes of read ffish butt nott houlsome, various sortes of small ffish for the Pann, good oysters and Crabes, Ells large and good.

"Herbage ffruite and Graine, ffrench or Cidney Beanes, Potatoes, sallating; Pumplemuses, oranges, Jumboes, Watter and musk Melones, Sugar Cannes, Pumkines, Tobacco that Hellish weed, and many other things forgotten."

The first authentic account of the Dodo is supposed to have been given by one Jacob Cornelius Van Neck, a Dutch navigator, who visited Mauritius in 1598, and finding it uninhabited, took possession of it. Many birds were found on the island; one of which was of strange appearance, and which they called "Walekvögel" (disgusting birds), and described as about the size of a Swan, having a larger head, with a sort of hood, wings replaced by a few black quills, and the tail represented by four or five grayish plumes.

Not having access to the manuscript, I again refer to Mr. Strickland's work on the Dodo, where he quotes Sir Hamon Lestrange's account of seeing a live bird of this species (Sloane MSS. 1839, 5, p. 9).

"About 1638 as I walked London streets, I saw the picture of a strange fowle hong out upon a cloth [hiatus in the MS.] and myself with one or two more then in company went in to see it. It was kept in a chamber, and was a great fowle somewhat bigger than the largest Turkey Cock, and so legged and footed, but shorter and thicker and of a more erect shape, coloured before like the breast of a young cock fesan, and on the back of dunn or deare coulour. The keeper called it a Dodo, and in the ende of a chymney in the chamber there lay a heape of large pebble stones, whereof hee gave it many in our sight, some as bigg as nutmegs, and the keeper told us shee eats them (conducing to digestion), and though I remember not how farr the keeper was questioned therein, yet I am confident that afterwards she cast them all againe."

It appears that Sir Thomas Herbert visited the island of Mauritius about 1627, and afterwards published several works on his travels, one of which was " A Relation of some yeares of Travaile begunne anno 1626 into Afrique and the greater Asia especially the territories of the Persian Monarchie and some parts of the Oriental Indies and Iles adjacent. By T. H. Esquire. Fol. London 1634." The following is an extract:—

" Furst here and here only and in Dygarroys, is generated the Dodo, which for shape and rarenesse may antigonize the Phœnix of *Arabia*: her body is round and fat, few weigh lesse than fifty pound, are reputed of more for wonder than food, greasie stomackes may seek after them, but to the delicate, they are offensive and of no nourishment.

" Her visage darts forth melancholy, as sensible of Nature's injurie in framing so great a body to be guided with complemental wings, so small and impotent, that they serue only to prove her *Bird*. The halfe of her head is naked, seeming couered with a fine vaile, her bill is crooked downwards, in midst is the thrill, from which part to the end tis of a light greene, mixt with a pale yellow tincture: her eyes are small, and like to Diamonds, round and rowling: her clothing downy feathers, her traine three small plumes, short and inproportionable, her legs suting to her body, her pounces sharpe, her appitite strong and greedy. Stones and Iron are degested, which description will better be conceiued in her representation."

After the colonization of the island of Mauritius, the Dodos gradually diminished in numbers; and we learn from Leguat, who visited the island in 1693, that many of the species which were once abundant had become quite rare. He says, " L'isle était autrefois toute remplie d'Oyes et de Canards sauvages; de Poules d'eau, de Gelinottes, de Tortues de mer et de terre: *mais tout cela est devenu fort rare.*" He makes no mention whatever of the Dodo: so that we may consider that it had become nearly or quite extinct at that time.

About the year 1712, Mauritius was colonized by the French under the name of the Isle de France. Since that date, we can find no record of its existence: and M. Morel, a French official, who lived there in 1778, says that the oldest inhabitants had no recollection of such birds.

The name *Dodo* was, in all probability, derived from the Dutch word *Dodoor*, meaning a sluggard, and would well apply, as the Dodo must have been slow and unwieldy in its movements. Sir T. Herbert, however, states that it is a Portuguese word; and as there is a word in that language (*Doudo*) meaning " foolish," it is possible that it may have been derived from either source.

The colors of the specimen figured in the plate are nearly the same as those of Savery's picture of the Dodo in the Royal Gallery at Berlin. Another picture, by the same artist, preserved in the Belvedere at Vienna, differs somewhat in general color, and has the plumes more yellow: but as some of the records distinctly say " grayish plumes," I have given them that color.

PTILORIS PARADISEUS.

PTILORIS PARADISEUS. *Swain.*

RIFLE BIRD.

Ptiloris paradiseus. — Swain, Zoöl. Journal, Vol. I. p. 481. — Gray, Gen. Birds, Vol. I. p. 94. — Cab. & Hein., Mus.
Hein., Theil I. p. 214. · · Reich., Hand. der Spec. Ornith. p. 328. — Gould, Birds of Austr., Vol. IV. pl. 100. —
Id., Hand. B. B. Austr., Vol. I. p. 591. — Elliot, Proc. Zoöl. Soc. 1871, p. 582. — Bonp., Comp. Gen. Av. 1850.
p. 412, sp. 1. · Less., Ois. Parad. 1835, syn. p. 25, sp. 1. — *Id.*, Hist. Nat, p. 23, pls. 29 and 30. — Elliot,
Mon. Parad., pl. 24.
Epimachus brisbani. — Wils., Ill. Zoöl., pl. 9. — Less., Man. Ornith., T. 11. pp. 6. 320.
Epimachus regius. — Less., Voy. Coquille, pl. 28. — *Id.*, Cent. Zoöl., pl. 3.
Epimachus paradiseus. — Schl., Mus. Pays-Bas, 1867, p. 97. — *Id.*, Journ. Ornith. 1861, p. 386.

HAB. — SOUTHEASTERN AUSTRALIA.

ALTHOUGH this beautiful species has been familiar to ornithologists for many years, yet, up to the present time, comparatively little has been learned regarding its habits. Birds of this family, until a short time ago, were unknown to Europeans in a living state: and it is only through the energy and perseverance of such men as Signor d'Albertis, Mr. Wallace, and a few others, that we have been able to obtain any definite information concerning them.

During the last century, many mutilated specimens of different species found their way into Europe, and a custom which the natives had of removing all traces of the legs in preparing the skins gave rise to the most extravagant stories concerning them. It was supposed that they had no feet, and never ceased floating about in the air. The name of the New Guinea species, *P. apoda*, shows that these ridiculous tales were not entirely discredited by the naturalists of that day.

Although wanting the flowing plumes, which so enhance the beauty of some of the other species of its family, the Rifle Bird is unsurpassed in richness of color; and if it is so beautiful in the cabinet, what must be its splendor as it flashes and glitters amid the tropical flowers of its native forests!

Mr. Gould, in his "Birds of Australia," gives a short account of this species. He says, "Hitherto, this magnificent bird has only been discovered in the bushes of the southeastern portions of Australia. So limited, in fact, does its range of habitat seem to be, that the river Hunter to the southward, and Moreton Bay to the eastward, may be considered its natural boundaries in either direction. I have been informed by several persons, who have seen it in its native wilds, that it possesses many habits in common with the *Chimacteri*, and that it ascends the upright boles of trees precisely after the manner of those birds. . . . The sexes offer the greatest possible difference in the coloring of their plumage: for, while the male is adorned with hues only equalled by some species of the *Trochilidæ*, or Humming-birds, the dress of the female is as sombre as can well be imagined. The law which exists whenever there is a great difference in the coloring of the sexes, causes many party-colored changes of plumage in the immature males during the period of moulting, which, however, during the first year, and probably for a longer period, cannot be distinguished from the females."

Adult Male. General Plumage. — Velvety black, but, when held in the light, showing bright lilac; feathers of the abdomen and flanks edged with olive green: feathers on top of the head and triangular throat-patch, small, and of a rich metallic bluish green: two central tail-feathers metallic green, the rest purplish black; bill and feet, black.

Adult Female. — Top of head dark brown, each feather showing a central line of buff; a superciliary line extending to the occiput, dull white; throat, yellowish white; upper parts, olive brown; primaries, brown, the edges of the webs showing bright rufous; tail, brown; underparts, buff, showing a shade of tawny, each feather having an irregular black V-shaped mark diagonal with the shaft; bill and feet, black.

Length 10.75; wing 6; tail 4; bill 1.88; tarsus 1.25.

I am indebted to Mr. D. G. Elliot for much valuable information regarding this species.
The figures represented in the plate are from specimens in my own collection.

APTERYX AUSTRALIS.

APTERYX AUSTRALIS. *Shaw.*

Native Name, "KIWI."

Apteryx australis.—Shaw, Nat. Misc., Vol. XXIV. pls. 1,037, 1,038; also Gen. Zoöl., Vol. XIII. pl. 71.—Less., Traité
d'Orn., p. 12.—Cuv., Regne Anim., T. I. p. 498.—Gould, Birds of Australia, Vol. VI. pl. 2.—Rowley, Ornith.
Misc., Vol. I. pl. 4 (juv.).—Yarrell, Trans. Zool. Soc., Vol. I. p. 71.—Owen, Art. Aves, Cycl. of Anat. and
Phys., Vol. I. 1836, p. 269; Trans. Zoöl. Soc., Vol. II. p. 257.—Ibis, (1862,) pp. 104, 233; (1870,) p. 523;
(1872,) pp. 35, 36, 414, 448; (1873,) pp. 447, 482; (1874,) p. 215; (1875,) pp. 261, 294.

IN the far-off islands of New Zealand there exists a family of birds known as the *Apterygidæ*, which are the smallest
living representatives of the so-called "wingless" birds, most of which are now no longer in existence. Four species
are known at the present time, and it is claimed that a fifth, larger than any as yet described, inhabits the mountains of the
interior; but no specimen of the latter has as yet been taken, although I have lately received a gigantic bird of this family
which may be the much sought after *A. maxima*. For our first information concerning the present species, we are indebted
to Dr. Shaw, who obtained his specimen from Capt. Barclay, of the ship "Providence," who brought it from New Zealand
about the year 1812. After his death, his then unique specimen passed into the possession of the Earl of Derby.

Owing to the energetic efforts of naturalists in later years, we have been able to obtain some information of its economy
and habits. It apparently has an aversion to sunlight, and keeps concealed in the thick undergrowth during the daytime;
but as soon as it is fairly dark, it wanders forth in search of food, probing the ground with its long bill for worms, which
appear to be its principal food. Generally, a number of these birds are found together, and, it is claimed, utter harsh cries
during their nocturnal expeditions.

Gould states that the favorite localities of this bird are those covered with extensive and dense beds of fern. He says:
"When hard pressed by dogs, the usual mode of chasing it, it takes refuge in crevices of the rocks, hollow trees, and in the
deep holes which it excavates in the ground in the form of a chamber. In these latter situations, it is said to construct its
nest of dried fern and grasses."

Mr. Short, in a letter to Mr. Yarrell (Glds. Bds. Austr.), says: "While undisturbed, the head is carried far back on
the shoulders, with the bill pointing to the ground; but when pursued, it runs with great swiftness, carrying the head
elevated like the Ostrich. It is asserted to be almost exclusively nocturnal in its habits, and it is by torchlight that it is
usually hunted by the natives, by whom it is sought after with the utmost avidity, the skins being highly prized for the
dresses of the chiefs; indeed, so much are they valued, that the natives can rarely be induced to part with them. The
feathers are also employed to construct artificial flies for the capture of fish, precisely after the European manner. When
attacked, it defends itself very vigorously, striking rapid and dangerous blows with its powerful feet and sharp spur, with
which it is also said to beat the ground in order to disturb the worms upon which it feeds, seizing them with its bill
the instant they make their appearance."

Mr. Potts writes (Trans. New Zealand Inst., Vol. II. p. 66, 1869): "An egg received at the Canterbury Museum from
Okarito, or its neighborhood, is believed to be an undoubted specimen of this species. It arrived in a fresh state in
November. It is white, much blunted at each end, and presented a very smooth surface. This enormous egg gives the
following measurements: Through the apis, 5 inches 1 line, with a breadth of 3 inches 4 lines."

The skin, according to the late Mr. Rowley, is so thick and tough that a pair of light shoes might easily be made of it, as it resembles leather, or the skin of a mammal, more than that of a bird.

The figure represented in the plate is from a specimen in my collection.

Adult Male. — Wing rudimentary, entirely concealed by feathers; entire body covered with long, hair-like feathers of a light brown color, edged with very dark brown and black; throat and face grayish, shading into the brown of the body; a number of long black hairs springing from the base of the upper mandible; nostril situated at the tip of the upper mandible, — a very curious feature; bill, yellowish horn color; feet, brown; iris, brown. The sexes are similar.

Length about 16; bill 4.30; tarsus 2.50.

CICINNURUS REGIUS.

CICINNURUS REGIUS. *Vieill.*

KING BIRD OF PARADISE

The King Bird of Paradise. — Edw., Birds, Vol. III. pl. 3 (1750).
Paradisea regia. — Linn., Syst. Nat. (1766), Vol. I. p. 166. — Gmel., Syst. Nat., Vol. I. pt. 1, pl. 400. — Lath., Ind. Ornith.,
    Vol. II. (1790), p. 194. — Shaw, Gen. Zoöl., Vol. VII. pt. 2 (1809), p. 497, pl. 67. — Less., Voy. Coquille
    (1826), pl. 26 (text), Vol. I. p. 688. — Cuv., Reg. Anim. (1829), Vol. I. p. 427. — Gray, Proc. Zoöl. Soc. (1858),
    p. 181, sp. 74 (1861), p. 436. — *Id.*, Hand-List of Birds, pt. 2 (1870), p. 16. — Wall., Proc. Zoöl. Soc. (1862),
    p. 160. — *Id.*, Ibis (1859), p. 111. — Gray, Gen. of Birds, Vol. II. p. 23, sp. 5. — Wall., Malay Archip., Vol. II.
    pp. 131, 248. — Schleg., Journ. für Ornith. (1861), p. 385.
Le Manucode. — Buff., Plan. Enlum. (1774), p. 192, t. 496. — Briss., Hist. des Ois., Vol. III. (1773), p. 163, pl. 13. —
    Levaill., Hist. Nat. des Ois., Parad. (1806). Vol. I. pls. 7, 8. — Vieill., Ois., Vol. II. (1802), pl. 5, p. 16.
Le Petit Oiseau de Paradis. — Briss., Ornith., Vol. II. p. 136, pl. 13 (1760).
Le Roi des Oiseaux de Paradis. — Sonnerat, Voy. Nouv. Guinée (1776), Vol. I. p. 156, pl. 95.
King Paradise Bird. — Lath., Gen. Syn., Vol. II. (1782), p. 475. — *Id.*, Gen. Hist. Birds, Vol. III. (1822), p. 188, sp. 5.
Cicinnurus spinturnix. — Less., Ois. Parad. (1835), Syn., p. 14, sp. 6. — *Id.*, Hist. Nat., p. 182, pls. 16, 17, 18.
Cicinnurus regius. — Vieill., Gal. des Ois., Vol. I. (1825), p. 146. — Less., Traité d'Orn. (1831), p. 338. — Wall., Ibis
    (1861), p. 287. - Shaw, Gen. Zoöl. (1826), Vol. XIV. p. 77. — Elliot, Mon. Parad. (1873). pl. 15. — Salvad.
    and D'Albert, Ann. Mus. Cir. Genoa (1875), p. 832. — Gould, Birds of New Guinea, pt. 3, pl. 9.
Cicinnurus regia. — Bonap., Consp. Gen. Av. (1851), p. 413, sp. 1. — Gray, List Gen. Bds. (1855), p. 65.

HAB. — NEW GUINEA, ARU ISLANDS.

THIS lovely little species has been well known to naturalists for many years, yet very little is known regarding its economy and habits. Although unsurpassed in brilliancy of plumage by any of its family, it is hardly entitled to the name of "*regius*," which has come down to us from the older authors. "*Spinturnix*," as it was called by Lesson, would have been much more applicable, as it can hardly claim the rank of king, when compared with such species as *Epimachus speciosus* or *Astrapia nigra.*

Mr. Wallace met with this species in the Aru Islands. He writes: "The first two or three days of our stay here were very wet, and I obtained but few insects or birds; but at length, when I was beginning to despair, my boy, Baderoon, returned one day with a specimen which repaid me for months of delay and expectation. It was a small bird, — a little less than the Thrush. Merely in arrangement of colors and texture of plumage, this little bird was a gem of the first water; yet these comprised only half its strange beauty. Springing from each side of the breast, and ordinarily lying concealed under the wings, were little tufts of grayish feathers about two inches long, and each terminated by a broad band of intense emerald green. These plumes can be raised at the will of the bird, and spread out into a pair of elegant fans when the wings are elevated. But this is not the only ornament. The two middle feathers of the tail are in the form of slender wires, about five inches long, and which diverged in a beautiful curve. About half an inch of the end of this wire is webbed on the outer side only, and colored of a fine metallic green; and being curled spirally inwards, they form a pair of elegant glittering buttons, hanging five inches below the body, and at the same distance apart.

These two ornaments — the breast fans and the spiral-tipped tail wires — are altogether unique, not occurring on any other species of the eight thousand different birds that are known to exist upon the earth; and, combined with the most exquisite beauty of plumage, render this one of the most perfectly lovely of the many lovely productions of nature. My transports of admiration and delight quite amused my Aru hosts, who saw nothing more in '*Burong raja*' than we do in the Robin or Goldfinch. Thus one of my objects in coming to the far East was accomplished. I had obtained a specimen of the King Bird of Paradise, which had been described by Linnæus from skins preserved in a mutilated state by the natives. I knew how few Europeans had ever beheld the perfect little organism I now gazed upon, and how very imperfectly it was still known in Europe. The emotions excited in the mind of a naturalist who has long desired to see the actual thing which he has hitherto known only by description, drawing, or badly preserved external covering, especially when that thing is of surpassing rarity and beauty, require the poetic faculty fully to express them. After the first King Bird was obtained, I went with my men into the forest, and we were not only rewarded with another in equally perfect plumage, but I was enabled to see a little of the habits of both it and a larger species. It frequents the lower trees of the less dense forest, and is very active, flying strongly with a whirring sound, and constantly flying from branch to branch. It eats hard, stone-bearing fruits as large as a gooseberry, and often flutters its wings after the manner of the South American Manakins, at which times it elevates and expands the beautiful fans with which its breast is adorned. The natives of Aru call it 'Goby-goby.' It is tolerably plentiful in the Aru Islands, which led to its being brought to Europe at an early period, along with *Paradisea apoda*. It also occurs in the island of Mysol, and in every part of New Guinea which has been visited by naturalists."

Since the publication of Mr. Wallace's article, Sig. d'Albertis has taken it at Mt. Epa. Specimens have also been procured in Salwatti, by Bernstein and Von Rosenberg, and on the opposite coast, at Sorong.

Adult Male. — Upper parts, including head and throat, fiery red, the feathers resembling spun glass, especially so upon the back; feathers covering the upper mandible for more than half its length, shading into a beautiful orange color; a small spot of very dark green over the eye; a broad band of iridescent green upon the breast, separated from the red of the throat by a fine line of golden-tipped feathers; a number of lengthened feathers from the sides under the wing. These feathers are gray, becoming pale buff near the ends, and tipped with metallic green. When spread, they resemble a fan. The rest of the under parts white; under tail feathers gray. Two shafts project from the tail feathers, extending about four inches; near the tip an outer web of bright green appears, which is coiled into the form of a button; bill, yellow; legs and feet, pale blue; iris, brown.

Length (not including the extended shafts) 6.50; wing 4; tail 1.70; tarsus 1.12; upper mandible, from feathers to tip, .45.

Adult Female. — Upper parts, including head, dark brown; under parts, buff, marked with dark brown; edges of tail feathers showing an olive tinge.

The young bird has the upper parts light brown; outer edges of secondaries, orange; under parts, buff; flanks and throat marked with dark brown.

The specimens represented in the plate are from birds in my collection.

ALCA IMPENNIS.

ALCA IMPENNIS. *Linn.*

GREAT AUK.

Alca impennis.—Linn., Syst. Nat., I. p. 210 (1766).— Shaw, General Zoology, XIII., Pt. 1, p. 51.—Latham, Birds, X. p. 55.—Audubon, Birds of America, VII. p. 265.—Gould, Birds of Europe, V. pl. 400. — Dresser, Hist. Birds of Europe, Pt. 79. —Ibis, (1859,) p. 174; (1860,) p. 300; (1861,) pp. 15, 374, 396; (1862,) pp. 77, 301, 381; (1864,) pp. 354, 356, 466; (1865,) pp. 116, 222, 228, 336, 450, 524; (1866,) pp. 223, 224; (1867,) p. 384; (1868,) pp. 342, 457, 483; (1869,) pp. 229, 358, 359, 360, 393; (1870,) pp. 256, 449, 450, 518; (1871,) pp. 431, 455; (1872,) p. 449.
Alca major.—Briss. Orn., VI. p. 85.
Le Grand Pingouin.—Buff., Hist. Nat. Ois., IX. p. 393.
Chenalopex impennis.—(L.) G. R. Gray, Hand-List Birds, III. p. 95.

AT the beginning of the present century the Great Auk was not uncommon along our northern shores; but at the present time, owing to the persecution of man, it has disappeared, and none have been seen alive for many years. Perhaps a few individuals may still linger amid the solitary fastnesses of the north. Some unknown bay affords them a secure hiding-place until they too shall have passed away, and the only trace of this noble bird will be a few dried skins in some of the museum collections. This species at one time seems to have been abundant on both sides of the Atlantic; but at the beginning of the present century its numbers had so decreased that it was common only among the small islands on the coast of Newfoundland and in the Gulf of St. Lawrence, where, on account of its total inability to fly, it became an easy prey to the fishermen who regularly visited its breeding-places and carried away large numbers of the birds and eggs. On the other side of the Atlantic it was also abundant, and bred among the Orkney and Faroe Islands, where it was well known at a comparatively recent date. We have records of its occurrence at St. Kilda as late as 1822.

According to Faber (Prodr. Isl. Orn.), the Great Auk bred commonly upon two isolated rocks in the sea south of Iceland, whither the natives, for more than a century, had made annual expeditions to procure the birds and eggs.

In the year 1813 a vessel from the Färöes landed there, and the men procured many specimens, twenty-four being sent to Rejkjavik. In 1830 a skin and one egg were sent to the Copenhagen Museum by Count Moltke, which he wrote had been obtained on the island of Eldey.

Mr. Dresser states (Hist. Birds of Europe, Pt. 79): " Between that year (1830) and 1844, as appears by Wolley's researches, not fewer than sixty birds were killed on this island. The last specimens known to have been taken on Eldey were killed in 1844, and having been skinned in Iceland, were sent with their bodies in spirit to Prof. Eschricht, at Copenhagen."

Latham's " General History of Birds" contains an interesting account of this species. He says: " This, as far as we can learn, is by no means a common species. It appears on the isle of St. Kilda the beginning of May, and retires in June, and probably breeds there. It lays one large egg close to the sea mark, about six inches long, white, irregularly marked with purplish lines, and blotched at the larger end with black or ferruginous spots, and it is said that if the egg is taken away the bird will not lay a second; is supposed to hatch late as in August; the young are only covered with gray down; it never ventures far out to sea, rarely beyond soundings. Sometimes frequents the coast of Norway, the Ferroe Isles, Iceland, and Greenland; feeds much on the lump fish, father lasher, and others of that size, but the young birds will frequently eat rose root (*rhodiola rosea*), and other plants. The old ones are rarely seen on shore, though the young ones are often met with. It is a shy bird, and from the situation of its legs, being placed far behind, walks badly, but dives well, and is taken in the manner used for the Razorbill and Puffin; the skin between the jaws is blown into a bladder, and in this state used attached to the darts of the Greenlanders. It inhabits also Newfoundland; and it is said that the skin of the body is used by the Eskimaux Indians for garments. This bird was found by Dr. Bullock during his summer excursion in 1813, in Papa Vestray, one of the Orkney Islands. It was sufficiently familiar with the boatmen about those parts, but would not admit of his coming as a stranger within gunshot, though in their company; but afterwards suffering the boatmen by themselves to approach so near as to knock it down with an oar. This specimen was in good preservation in Mr. Bullock's museum. The sexes of this species are called King and Queen of Auks, and by some Gair-fowls."

Audubon, in writing of the Great Auk, says: "The only authentic account of the occurrence of this bird on our coasts that I possess was obtained from Mr. Henry Havell, brother of my engraver, who, when on his passage from New York to England, hooked a Great Auk on the banks of Newfoundland, in extremely boisterous weather. On being hauled on board, it was left at liberty on the deck. It walked very awkwardly, often tumbling over; bit every one within reach of its powerful bill, and refused food of all kinds. After continuing several days on board, it was restored to its proper element."

He also says the fishermen in Labrador assured him that the Penguin, as they name this bird, bred on a low, rocky island to the southeast of Newfoundland, where they destroyed great numbers of the birds and eggs. The female deposited a single egg upon the bare rock, somewhat resembling that of *Uramania torda*, but larger, and changeable in its coloration. It usually measures about 4.85 by 2.70.

Prof. A. Newton, in the "Ibis" for 1870, pp. 256, 261, gives a most careful list of the skins, skeletons, and eggs known to be in existence. Of skins, Germany has 20; Denmark, 2; France, 7 or 8; Holland, 2; Italy, 5; Norway, 1; Sweden, 2; United Kingdom, 22; Russia, 1; Switzerland, 3; Belgium, 2; Portugal, 1; United States, 3.

Mr. D. G. Elliot, to whom my thanks are due for many valuable notes, writes me that he purchased one example in London for Mr. Robert L. Stuart, which that gentleman presented to the Natural History Museum in Central Park, New York. This reduces the number in the United Kingdom to 21, and gives 4 to the United States.

Of skeletons, Germany has 1; France, 1; Italy, 1; United Kingdom, 4; and the United States, 2. It appears that there are also a number of detached bones. Of these, Denmark has the remains of 10 or 11 specimens; Norway has 8 or 10; the United Kingdom, 13; and the United States, 7. Of eggs, Germany has 8; Belgium, 2; Denmark, 1; France, 7; Holland, 2; United Kingdom, 41; Switzerland, 2; United States, 2. We know, therefore, of the existence of 71 or 72 skins; 9 skeletons; 63 eggs; and the detached bones of 41 different birds.

Adult in Summer.—Head and upper parts, wings, and tail black, sometimes faintly tinged with brown on the neck; a large oval white spot in front of the eye; secondaries tipped with white; breast and under parts white; legs and beak black; mandible deeply furrowed; iris brown.

Length about 30; wing 6; tail 2; tarsus 2.14; beak 3.60.

Adult in Winter.—Described by some authors as having the chin and front of the neck white. Figured by Donivan from the Leverian Museum specimen.

Young.—Said to be similar to the adult; but has fewer furrows on the lower mandible. (*Newcastle Museum.*)

The specimen figured in the plate is an adult bird in full summer plumage, now in the British Museum.

MENURA SUPERBA

MENURA SUPERBA. *Davies.*

LYRE BIRD.

Menura superba.— Davies, Linn. Trans., Vol. VII. p. 207, pl. 22.— Lath., Ind. Orn. Supp., p. 61.— Shaw, Gen. Zoöl.,
    Vol. XIV. p. 313.— Gould, Birds of Austr., Vol. III. pl. 14.
Le Parkinson.— Vieill, Ois. de Parad., pls. 14, 15, 16.
Megapodius menura.— Wagl., Sys. Av., sp. 1.
Menura lyra.— Shaw, Nat. Misc., pl. 577.— Vieill. Gal. des Ois., pl. 192.— G. R. Gray, List of Gen. of Birds, p. 71.
Menura Novæ-Hollandiæ.— Lath., Ind. Orn. Supp., p. 61. — Temm., Man., T. I. p. 50.— Less, Traite d'Orn., p. 478, pl. 88.
Menura paradisea.— Swain, Class. of Birds, Vol. II. p. 351.
Superb Menura.— Lath., Gen. Syn., Vol. II. p. 271.— *Ib.*, Gen. Hist., Vol. VIII. p. 159, pl. 124.

THIS strange species is a native of Australia, where it seems to be restricted to the interior of New South Wales. It is eagerly sought after by the natives, who use the tail feathers in the manufacture of their ornaments. Being very shy, and frequenting an almost inaccessible portion of the country, it is not strange that perfect birds are rather difficult to obtain. All the naturalists who have visited that country agree that it is only by great care and perseverance that they have been able to procure specimens.

According to those who have seen the Lyre Bird in a wild state, it rarely, if ever, leaves the ground, but trusts entirely to its powers of running to escape its pursuers. Many expedients are resorted to by the hunters to procure it. It is said that if suddenly startled by the sight of a dog, it will take to the branches of a tree, and while its attention is attracted by the barking of the dog it may be easily shot. Sometimes the tail of an adult bird is fastened to the hat of the hunter, and while passing cautiously through the thick brush, a male will sometimes show itself while endeavoring to obtain a view of what it supposes to be another of its species.

Gould, in writing of this species, says: "Although upon one occasion I forced this bird to take wing, it was merely for the purpose of descending a gully, and I am led to believe that it seldom exerts this power unless under similar circumstances. It is particularly partial to traversing the trunks of fallen trees, and frequently attains a considerable altitude by leaping from branch to branch. Independently of its loud, full call, which may be heard reverberating over the gullies to the distance of at least a quarter of a mile, it possesses an inward and varied song, the lower notes of which can be heard when you have successfully approached to within a few yards of the bird during the time it is singing. This animated strain is frequently discontinued abruptly, and again commenced with a low, inward, snapping noise, ending with an imitation of the loud and full note of the Satin Bird, and always accompanied with a tremulous motion of the tail. The food of the *Menura* appears to consist principally of insects, particularly centipedes and coleoptera. I also found the remains of shelled snails in the gizzard, which is very strong and muscular."

It is claimed that the Lyre Bird lays two eggs of a light color, covered with small red spots. The nest is a large, rough structure, generally built upon a rock or trunk of a fallen tree.

Adult male.— Head slightly crested; general plumage brown, the secondaries and upper tail coverts showing reddish brown; a tinge of rufous on the throat; underparts grayish, palest on the vent; tail composed of sixteen feathers, very long, and shaped in the form of a lyre; the upper surface of the feathers dark brown, the under surface silvery gray; a band of dark brown at the tips of the large outer feathers. These feathers are marked by numerous perfectly transparent bands, the edges of the inner webs showing alternately pale rufous and dark brown, the two central feathers crossing in a graceful curve near the extremity and showing a narrow inner web, the rest covered with long hair-like filaments, giving the whole a graceful and beautiful appearance, unequalled by any other known form; bare space of the eye, lead color; legs and feet, black; irides, dark brown.

Length about 3 feet; wing about 11.30; tail about 25; tarsus 4.40; bill 1.25; mid. toe and claw 3.

The female differs from the male in wanting the ornamental tail, the feathers being webbed in the usual manner and shorter. The bare space around the eye is also somewhat smaller, and the general plumage duller.

DIPHYLLODES RESPUBLICA. *Bonap.*

WILSON'S BIRD OF PARADISE.

Lophorina respublica. — Honap., Compt. Rend. (1850), p. 131.
Diphyllodes respublica. — Bonap., Comp. (1850), p. 413; Sclater, P. Z. S., 1857, p. 6; Von Rosenb., Journ. für Ornith.
    (1864), p. 130; Elliot, Monogr. Parad. (1873), pl. 14; Gould, Bds. New Guinea (1876), Pt. 3.
Paradisea wilsoni. — Cass., Journ. Acad. Nat. Scien. Phil. (1850), Vol. II. p. 15; Gray, P. Z. S., 1861, p. 436; Sclater,
    P. Z. S., 1865, p. 465; Schleg., Mus. Pays-Bas (1867), p. 87.
Schlegia calva. -- Bernst., Nederl. Tijds. Dierk. (1864), Pt. 1, pl. 7.
Diphyllodes wilsoni. — Wall., P. Z. S., 1862, p. 160; Newton. *Ibis*, 1865, p. 343; Wall., Malay Arch. (1869), Vol. II. p. 248.

HAB. — BATANA AND WAIGIOU ISLANDS.

THIS curious species was described by Prince Bonaparte, in February, 1850, antedating the late Mr. Cassin, of Philadelphia, who also described it in August of the same year.

Although more than thirty years have passed since it was first made known to science, almost nothing is known regarding the economy and habits of this species. Dr. Bernstein was the first naturalist who had the pleasure of seeing it alive, and he procured a fine series from the islands of Batana and Waigiou, where he found it not uncommon in the interior. In his original notes concerning it, he gave it the rank of a new genus, on account of the peculiar appearance of the skull; but both Mr. Elliot and the late Mr. Gould placed it in the present genus, and in my opinion, with our present system of classification, the bare tracts of the skull, without other characteristic differences, is not sufficient to admit of its generic separation.

Adult Male. — Head bare, crossed by narrow lines of short, blackish purple feathers; skin blue, showing a tinge of green near the feathers; nuchal crest, bright yellow; mantle crimson, bordered with black; wings brown, the feathers edged with crimson, — some of the tertials almost entirely of that color; underparts lustrous green, becoming purplish black on the throat and head; belly, dark purplish brown; tail brownish, two long feathers of a rich purplish tinge springing from the base of the tail, crossing in a graceful curve, webbed only on one side, and resembling in form the figure 6; bill black; legs and feet bluish; iris, reddish brown.

Length 6; wing 4; tail 1.50; tarsus 1.10; bill .50.

Adult Female. — Head bare, as in the male; above, dull olive; wings and tail, brown, tinged with rufous, brightest on the secondaries and tertiaries; underparts pale yellowish, barred with narrow brown lines. Somewhat smaller than the male, and wanting the elongated tail feathers.

The specimens figured in the plate are from an adult male and female in my collection.

MACHETES PUGNAX.

MACHETES PUGNAX. *(L.)* Cuv.

RUFF.

Tringa pugnax.—Linn., Syst. Nat. (1766), Vol. I. p. 247.
Le Chevalier varie.—Buff., Hist. Nat. Ois. (1780), Vol. VII. p. 517.
Tringa equestris.—Lath., Ind. Orn. (1790), Vol. II. p. 730.
Tringa rufescens.—Bechst., Gemeinn. Naturg. Deutschl. (1809), Vol. III. p. 332.
Totanus pugnax (L.).—Nilss., Orn. Suec. (1817), Vol. II. p. 71.
Machetes, Cuv. (Tringa pugnax, L.).—Règ. Animal. (1817), Vol. I. p. 490.
Machetes pugnax (L.).—C. L. Brehm (1831), Vög. Deutschl., p. 670.—Shaw, Gen. Zoöl., Vol. XII. p. 110.—Gould,
    Bds. of Europe, Vol. IV. pl. 325.—Degland et Gerbe, Ornith. Européenne, T. II. p. 211.—Dresser, Hist. Bds.
    of Europe, pt. 69.—Coues, Key N. A. Birds, p. 260.—Shelly, Bds. of Egypt, p. 246.
Limosa hardwickii.—J. E. Gray, Ill. Ind. Zoöl. (1835), Vol. II. p. 52.
Philomachus pugnax (L.).—G. R. Gray, List Gen. Birds (1841), p. 89.—Cassell, Book Bds, Vol. IV. p. 39.
Machetes minor.—C. L. Brehm, Vogelfang (1855), p. 320.

THE Ruff, as the male bird of this curious species is called, has a very extended range, being distributed over the whole of Europe, Africa, and the greater part of Asia, where it has been taken as far east as Kamtschatka. Specimens have also been recorded from the United States, but instances of its actual capture on our shores are of rare occurrence.

In Africa it is abundant in winter, and the greater part of the birds are probably winter visitants, although Von Heuglin says that he observed the Ruff in Northeast Africa during the breeding season, and states that he killed specimens in July and August near the bitter lakes of Suez. During the months of February and March, I have found it common in the vicinity of Lake Menzaleh and the Fayoom. It has also been observed in Abyssinia at an altitude of ten thousand feet.

At the commencement of the breeding season the males collect, apparently to fight for the possession of the females. They are very fierce, and show great ardor during their battles, but it is claimed that they rarely injure one another to any extent. These engagements take place on rising ground, or small hill, and the males return to the same place each morning to renew the contest. The knowledge of this habit is of great advantage to the fowler, who, upon finding one of these battle-grounds, spreads his net, places his decoys, and rarely fails to capture a number of the birds.

Shaw, writing of this species, gives an interesting account of its pugnacious disposition (Shaw, Gen. Zoöl., Vol. XII. p. 112). He says: "The most remarkable circumstance attending the history of this species is its quarrelsome disposition, which is said to arise from the number of males greatly exceeding that of the females, as upon their arrival in this country in the spring, the males each fix upon a small hillock or dry, grassy spot in the marshes, about which he runs around till he has almost trodden the space bare, and the moment a female comes in sight, all the males within a certain distance commence a general battle, placing their beaks on the ground, spreading the feathers of the neck, and using the same action as a cock; and their combats are described as both desperate and of long continuance, but at the end the female generally becomes the prize of the victor. . . . An erroneous opinion prevails that the fattening of Ruffs, when in confinement, should take place in the dark, lest the admission of light should set them to fighting; the fact is, that every bird, even when kept in a room, takes its stand as it would in the open air, and if another invades its circle a battle ensues. A whole roomful of them may be set into fierce contest by compelling them to shift their stations; but after the cause has subsided, they resume their circles and become pacific. In confinement they do not lose their pugnacious disposition; and if a basin of bread and milk or boiled wheat is set before them, it is instantly contended for, and they would starve in the midst of plenty if several dishes of food were not placed among them at a distance from each other."

Although a polygamous species, it is claimed that the male attaches himself more especially to one female, and shows a decided preference for her. The food consists of insects, grasshoppers, worms, etc. They are very easily tamed, and in captivity become almost omnivorous. The nest is placed on the ground, generally near a marsh, and is concealed with great care. The eggs are four in number, of a dull, buff color, marked with rich brown, and usually measure about 1.70 x 1.20, but like those of other waders they vary in size.

Adult male (spring plumage). — Feathers of the head and neck elongated, forming a wide collar or ruff, generally white and buff; rest of upper parts variegated with buff, black, dull white, and ochre; primaries dark brown, with white shafts; underparts white, heavily marked with blackish brown on the breast and sides; face covered with yellowish tubercles; bill, dark brown, lighter at the base; iris, dark brown; legs, brownish yellow.

Length 12.5; wing 7; tail 2.7; tarsus 2; bill 1.55.

Male winter plumage. — Lacking the ruff and tubercles on the face, resembles the female.

Adult female. (Reeve.) Head and neck sandy brown, mottled faintly with dark brown; upper parts variegated with black and brown and tinge of reddish; underparts dull white, mottled on the breast and sides with brown. The rest as in the male; no ruff or tubercles on the face. Smaller than the male.

The specimens figured in the plate represent two adult males and a female. The variation in the coloration of the plumes of the former is very great. The Ruff may be black, white, or chestnut, barred and banded in various ways, or simply plain white, generally showing a tinge of buff or black.

PSEUDOGRYPHUS CALIFORNIANUS.

PSEUDOGRYPHUS CALIFORNIANUS. (*Shaw.*)

CALIFORNIA CONDOR.

Vultur californianus.—Shaw, Nat. Misc., Vol. IX. pl. 301 (1797); Lath., Ind. Orn., Suppl. 2; Dougl., Zoöl. Journ., Vol. IV. p. 328; Wils, Vol. IV. p. 259.

Cathartes californianus.—Cuv., Reg. Animal., Vol. I. p. 316; Bonap., Syn., p. 22 (1828); DeKay, Zoöl. N. Y., Vol. II. p. 3 (1844); Nutt., Man., Vol. I. p. 39 (1833); Aud., Bds. N. A., pl. 426; Orn. Biog., Vol. V. p. 240; Cassin, Bds. N. Am., p. 5 (1858); Heerm., P. R. R. Rept., Vol. II. p. 29 (1855); Gray, Hand List, Vol. I. p. 3 (1869); Taylor, Hutchins' Cala. Mag., Vol. III. p. 537 (1859); Gurney, Cat. Rapt Bds., p. 39 (1864); Sclater, P. Z. S., p. 366 (1866), p. 183 (1868); Coues, Key, p. 222 (1872); Bds. N. W., p. 384 (1874).

Sarcorhamphus californianus.—Step., Zoöl., XIII. p. 6 (1815); Rich and Swain's F. B. A., Vol. II. p. 1 (1831); Licht., Orn. Calif., p. 8.

Cathartes vulturinus.—Yeturn., Pl. 31 (1820); Lesa, Man. Orn., Vol. VII. p. 10 (1828).

Pseudogryphus californianus.—Bd., Bwr., and Ridg., N. Am. Bds., Vol. III. p. 338 (1874).

HAB.—PACIFIC COAST OF THE UNITED STATES FROM COLUMBIA RIVER TO LOWER CALIFORNIA. UTAH (Henshaw). ARIZONA (Coues).

THE California Vulture is of immense size, very nearly equalling in its dimensions the far-famed Condor of South America (*Sarcorhamphus gryphus*).

This interesting species was at one time very abundant in some parts of California, but of late years it has become a very rare bird,—in all probability its days are numbered. It is claimed that its destruction has been mainly caused by feeding upon the poisoned meat which had been left by the settlers to kill bears and other wild animals which at that time infested the country. Owing to its present scarcity, the California Vulture will soon be much sought after, large prices will be offered for specimens, and they will be killed at every opportunity. Gradually they will become fewer and fewer, until the day shall come when the report of some collector's gun will sound the death-knell of the last living representative of its race.

According to Dr. Heermann, this Vulture was often observed sailing majestically in wide circles at a great height. Often when hunting in the Tejon Valley they would see no specimens for hours; but as soon as game was killed, these birds would be seen rising above the horizon before the body had grown cold. He also states that he has known them to devour a deer within an hour, and that four of them dragged the body of a young grizzly bear, that weighed over a hundred pounds, the distance of two hundred yards.

According to Dr. Cooper, this species visits the Columbia River in autumn, and feeds upon the dead salmon which are found along its shores. The flight is described as slow, steady, and very graceful, and they sail along with no perceptible motion of the wings.

Mr. Alexander S. Taylor, of Monterey, published a series of papers on the Vulture (*vide* Bd., Bwr., and Ridg., Bds. N. A., p. 342, Vol. III.). He states that a Mexican *ranchero*, hunting among the highest peaks of the Santa Lucia Range, disturbed two pairs of these birds from their breeding places. There was no nest, the eggs having been deposited in the hollow of a tall old *robles* oak, in a steep *barranca*, near the summit of one of the highest peaks. He brought back with him from one a young bird only a few days old; and from the other an egg which was of a dull white color, the surface of the shell slightly roughened. It measured 4.50 inches in length, by 2.38 in diameter. The young Vulture was of an ochreous-yellow color, covered with a fine down of dull white.

Although rare, there is no doubt that the California Vulture is still to be found in some localities. Mr. W. E. Bryant, of San Francisco, writes me that he has seen two or three specimens while on hunting expeditions during the past year.

The following description of an adult specimen is taken from Bd., Bwr. and Ridg., N. A. Birds:—

"*Adult.*—Bill, yellowish white; naked skin of the head and neck, orange and red; iris, carmine (authors). General plumage dull black, the upper surface with a faint bluish lustre, the feathers (excepting the primary coverts, secondary coverts, and remiges) passing into dull brownish on their margins, producing a squamate appearance; scapulars and (more appreciably) the secondaries and their coverts with a hoary, grayish cast, the latter white for most of their exposed portions (producing a band across the wing), the white following the edges of the secondaries nearly to the ends; primaries and tail feathers, with their shafts, uniform deep black; whole lining of the wing (except the outer border) and axillaries, pure white; lower parts continuous dull, carbonaceous black, the tips of the pencillate feathers with a hoary or chalky tinge."

Young.—Bill, dusky; skin of the head dark, partly covered with a soft gray down. Entire plumage duller than in the adult, the white being mostly absent.

Wing 33; tail about 15; tarsus 5.10; bill (nostril to tip) 2.60.

The specimen figured in the plate is an immature bird in my collection. An adult is represented in the background.

ASTRAPIA NIGRA. *Bonap.*

INCOMPARABLE BIRD OF PARADISE.

Gorget Paradise Bird.—Lath., Gen. Syn., I. p. 478, pl. 20 (1782).
Paradisea nigra.—Gmel., Syst. Nat., Vol. I. p. 401 (1788).
Paradisea gularis.—Lath., Ind. Ornith., Vol. II. p. 196 (1790); Shaw, Gen. Zoöl., Vol. VII. p. 501 (1809).
La Pie de Paradis, ou l'incomparable Leraill.—Hist. Nat. Ois. Parad., Vol. I. (1806).
Le Hausse-col doré.—Vieill., Ois. Dor., Vol. II. (1802).
Epimachus niger.—Schleg., Mus. Pays-Bas, p. 94 (1867).
Astrapia gularis.—Vieill., Gal. des Ois., Tom. I. p. 109, pl. 107 (1825); Less., Trait. Ornith., p. 338 (1831); Von Rosenb., Journ. für Ornith., p. 131 (1864); Less., Ois Parad., p. 18, sp. 8 (1835).
Astrapia nigra.—Bonap., Consp. Gen. Av., p. 414 (1850); Gray, Gen. Birds, Vol. II. p. 326; Wall., Proc. Zoöl. Soc. (1862), pp. 154, 155, 159, 160; Shaw, Gen. Zoöl., Vol. XIV. (1826); Wall., Malay Archipel., Vol. II. p. 257; Elliot, Mon. Parad., pl. 9 (1873); Salvad., Ann. Mus. Cir. Genov., IX. p. 190 (1876); Sharpe, Cat. Bds. Brit. Mus., III. p. 165 (1877); Gould, Bds. New Guinea, Pt. VIII. (1878).

HAB.—NEW GUINEA.

THIS magnificent species inhabits the high mountains in the interior of New Guinea, and the slight accounts which we have of its economy and habits are due to the energy of a few naturalists who, within the last few years, have succeeded in penetrating into the interior.

Dr. Beccari procured several specimens in the Arfak Mountains. He says : "Epimachus maximus and Astrapia gularis are only found on the highest and most difficult peaks of Mount Arfak, nearly always above six thousand feet elevation. Specimens in dark plumage are common enough, but those which have attained perfect plumage are rare, perhaps because they take some years to acquire it. Both of them live on the fruits of certain Pandanaceæ, and especially on those of the Freycinetiæ, which are epiphytous on the trunks of trees. The irides of the large Epimachus are dark brick-red ; those of the Astrapia almost black. The neck feathers of the latter are erectible, and expand into a magnificent collar round the head. The first day I went out at Atam, on June 23, I got both these species (two specimens of each), besides one Drepanoris albertisi, three Paradigallæ, one Parotia, and several other wonderful kinds of birds. It was a memorable day; because I ascended one of the peaks, and was surprised to find myself surrounded by four or five species of vaccinium and rhododendron. I also found an umbellifer (a drymis), and various other plants common to the mountains of Java, and there were also some mosses a foot and a half in height."

Adult male.—General plumage above, velvety black with a purplish tinge; wings black, with tinge of purple, the inner primaries cut squarely at the tips; two central tail feathers very long, showing magnificent purple when held to the light; feathers of the head black, of a velvety texture, the top of the head showing steel-blue reflections; nape covered by a shield of golden-green feathers. From each side of the latter springs a ruff of velvety black; a band of brilliant golden copper-color from behind the eye, down the neck, and encircling the throat; under surface rich green; the lateral plumes of the breast tipped with metallic green; bill and feet, black; iris, very dark brown.

Adult female.—Much smaller. General plumage black; the inner edges of secondaries rufous; outer edges of primaries narrowly edged with rufous; tail brownish black, faintly banded in some lights; underparts sometimes delicately lined with ash.

Length 28; wing 8.5; tail, including central feathers, 18.50; tarsus 1.50; bill 1.25.

The plate represents a male and female in my collection.

CAMPTOLAEMUS LABRADORIUS.

CAMPTOLÆMUS LABRADORIUS. *Gmel.*

LABRADOR DUCK.

Anas labradora.—Gm., Syst. Nat., I. 587 (1788); Lath., Ind. Orn., II. 859 (1790); Wils., Am. Orn., Vol. VIII.
p. 91 (1814).
Anas (Fuligula) labradora.—Bp., Obs. Wils. (1835).
Fuligula labradora.—Bp., Syn., 391 (1828); Nutt., Man., Vol. II. p. 428 (1834); Aud., Bds. N. Am., Vol. VI. p. 329,
pl. 400 (1843); DeKay, N. Y., p. 326 (1844); Schleg., Mus. Pays-Bas, Vol. VIII. (1865).
Rhynchaspis labradora.—Steph., Gen. Zoöl., XII. p. 121 (1824).
Camptolæmus labradorius.—Gray, List Gen. Bds. (1840); Reich., Syst. Ar., VIII. (1852); Coues, Proc. A. N. S. Phil., 329
(1861); Verr., Proc. Ess. Inst., III. 158 (1862); Coues, Key N. A. Bds., 291 (1872); Bds. N. W., p. 579 (1874).
Somateria labradoria.—Rowley, Ornith. Misc., Vol. II. p. 205.

HAB.—EASTERN COAST OF THE UNITED STATES, NORTHWARD—ARCTIC AMERICA?

IT is now many years since a specimen of the Labrador Duck is known to have been taken, and on account of its
disappearance, many naturalists have advanced the statement that it has ceased to exist, and joined the long list of species
known to science whose names are followed by the simple legend "extinct." That the Labrador Duck is no longer represented by living specimens I do not believe. That it is no longer to be found in localities where it was once abundant is
unquestionably true; but that does not argue its extinction. According to all accounts it was an extremely hardy bird,
frequenting the coast of New England during the coldest months of winter, and it seems plausible that this bird will yet be
found, together with many new and undescribed species, in the far-off and little-known regions of the north.

Audubon, in writing of this species, says, "It is a very hardy bird, and is met with along the coasts of Nova Scotia,
Maine, and Massachusetts during the most severe cold of winter. My friend, Prof. MacCulloch, has procured
several in his immediate neighborhood; and the Hon. Daniel Webster, of Boston, sent me a fine pair killed by himself in
the Vineyard Islands, on the coast of Massachusetts. . . . The range of this species along our shores does not extend
further southward than Chesapeake Bay, where I have seen some, near the influx of the St. James River. I have also met
with several in the Baltimore market. Along the coast of New Jersey and Long Island it occurs in greater or less number
every year. It also, at times, enters the Delaware River, and ascends it at least as far as Philadelphia. . . . The Pied Duck
seems to be a truly marine bird, seldom entering rivers unless urged by stress of weather. It procures its food by diving
amidst the rolling surf, over sand or mud bars; although at times it comes along the shore and searches in the manner of
the Spoon-bill Duck. Its usual fare consists of small shellfish, fry, and various kinds of seaweeds, along with which it
swallows much sand and gravel. Its flight is swift, and its wings emit a whistling sound. It is usually seen in flocks of
from seven to ten, probably the members of one family."

The following list of specimens is taken from Rowley's "Ornithological Miscellany," Vol. II. In the American list I
have made some slight alterations, in instances where the specimens are known to have changed hands:—

LIST OF SPECIMENS.

	Sex.	Number.
EUROPE.		
The British Museum	♂ ♀	3
♂ adult presented to the Museum by the Hudson's Bay Company, about the year 1835.		
♀ adult, purchased from Verreaux in 1863 with a miscellaneous lot of North American birds.		
Liverpool Museum	♂ ♀, ♂ juv.	3
♂ adult, purchased from Mr. Gould, Jan. 16, 1833.		
♀ adult, presented by T. C. Eyton, Esq.; purchased from Mr. Gould, Jan. 16, 1833.		

♂.—Though regarded by Lord Derby as a female, this would appear to be a young male, "for the
throat and breast are assuming the white of the male."

	Sex.	Number.
Strickland Collection, Cambridge	♂	1
Obtained by Mr. H. E. Strickland, from his relation, Mr. Arthur Strickland, in 1850, in full plumage and good condition. Nothing more is known about it.		
Col. Wedderburn's Collection	♂	1
Shot by him, in 1852, in Halifax Harbor. Sternum in Cambridge Museum.		
Leyden Museum	♂ ♀	2
Were obtained in 1863. The name put to them is "Prince of Neuwied."		
Berlin Museum	(?)	1
Paris Museum d'Histoire Naturelle	♂	1
Presented, in 1810, by Mr. Hyde; feet somewhat decayed.		

AMERICA.

Prof. Baird's List.

	Sex.	Number.
American Museum, Central Park, New York . . .	♂ ♂, ♂ juv., ♀	4
♂ adult, from the Wied Collection — "Labrador."		
♂ adult, from Mr. Elliot's Collection, Long Island, New York.		
♂ juv., " " " " "		
♀ adult, " " " " "		
Collection of Mr. George N. Lawrence	♂ ♀, ♂ juv.	3
♂ adult, obtained about 1842, Long Island, New York.		
♀ adult, " " " " "		
♂ juv., obtained about 1865.		
Long Island Historical Society	♂	1
♂ adult, 1842, Long Island, New York.		
Collection of Dr. Aiken	♂ juv.	1
♂ juv., obtained within a few years from Long Island, New York.		
Poughkeepsie, New York, — Vassar College	♂ ♀	
♂ adult, from collection of Mr. J. P. Giraud, Long Island.		
♀ adult, " " " "		
Albany, New York, — State Collection	♂	1
♂ adult, Long Island, New York.		
Burlington (Vermont University) .	♂ ♀	2
♂ adult, Long Island.		
♀ adult, "		
Philadelphia Academy of Natural Sciences	♂ ♀	2
Washington: Smithsonian Institute . . .	♂ ♂ ♀	3
♂, from Long Island.		
♀ and ♂, from Mr. Audubon's Collection. Locality unknown.		
Collection of Mr. William Brewster, Cambridge, Mass. . .	♀	1
Collection of Mr. Charles B. Cory, Boston, Mass. .	♂ ♀	2
Total		33

Adult male. — Head, neck, upper breast, and wing surface, including scapulars, wing coverts, and secondaries, white; a collar around the neck, and a stripe extending from the forehead along the top of the head to the base of the skull, black; rest of plumage, including upper back, primaries, and underparts, black; legs and toes ashy; webs black; terminal half of bill, black; basal half, pale orange, the latter color extending along the edges of the mandibles for two thirds the length of the bill; iris, dark hazel.

Adult female. — General plumage, brownish ash, with a bluish tinge on the feathers of the back and wing coverts; secondaries, white, forming a wing band; tertiaries, ashy, edged with black; bill and feet as in the male.

Length about 19; wing 8.25; tail 2.15; tarsus 1.95; bill 1.45.

The specimens figured in the plate are a male and female in my collection.

EPIMACHUS SPECIOSUS. *(Bodd.)*

MAGNIFICENT BIRD OF PARADISE.

Le Grand Promèrops de la Nouvelle-Guinee.—Sonn., Voy. Nov.-Guin., p. 163. pl. 101.
Grand Promèrops à paremens frisés.—Buff., H. N. Ois., Vol. VI. p. 472.
Upupa speciosa.—Bodd, Tabl., pl. enl., p. 39.
New Guinea Brown Promèrops.—Lnth., Gen. Syn. 1. Pt. 2. p. 694.
Promérops striata.—Shaw, Gen. Zoöl., Vol. VIII. p. 144.
Promérops superbus.—Shaw, tom. cit. p. 145.
Falcinellus superbus.—Vieill., N. D. d'Hist. Nat. 28, p. 166.
Epimachus magnus.—Cuv., Règne Anim., Vol. I. p. 407.
Cinnamolegus papuensis.—Less., Ois. Parad. Syn. p. 32.
Epimachus speciosus.—Gray, Gen. B. 1, p. 94.—Elliot, Mon. Parad., pl. 19.—Salvad., Ann. Mus. Civic. Genov., Vol. VII. p. 785; Vol. IX. p. 190.—Sharpe, Cat. B. 3, p. 162.—Gould, Bds. N. Guinea, Pt. VII.
Epimachus magnus.—Wall., *Ibis*, 1861, p. 287. - *Id.*, P. Z. S., 1862, p. 160.
Epimachus maximus.—Gray, P. Z. S., 1861, p. 433.—*Id.*, Handb. Bds. 1, p. 105.—Beccari, Am. Mus. Civic. Genov. 7, p. 710.—*Id.*, *Ibis*, 1876, p. 249.

ALTHOUGH the present species has been known to naturalists for many years, yet very little has been learned regarding it. Mr. Wallace did not find it during his explorations among the Papuan Islands. He says: "This splendid bird inhabits the mountains of New Guinea, in the same district with the Superb (*Lophorina atra*) and the Six-Shafted (*Parotia sexpennis*) Paradise Birds, and I was informed is sometimes found in the ranges near the coast. I was several times assured by different natives that this bird makes its nest in a hole under ground or among rocks, always choosing a place with two apertures, so that it may enter at one and go out at the other. This is very unlike what we should suppose to be the habits of the bird, but it is not easy to conceive how the story originated if it is not true; and all travellers know that the native accounts of animals, however strange they may seem, almost invariably turn out to be correct."

Adult Male. — Above brownish-black, showing steely reflections: upper part of head bright metallic blue; a line of steel-blue feathers down the middle of the back; quills brownish-black, showing bluish tinge in some lights; cheeks metallic blue, showing a purplish tinge in some lights; chin blackish; throat purple; underparts dark olive green. From the sides of the breast spring long feathers with broad outer webs, the inner webs being very narrow; these feathers are purplish-black, the lower ones tipped with brilliant metallic blue. The flank feathers, extending beyond the lateral plumes, are broadly tipped with brilliant emerald-green, preceded by a narrow line of blue. Two central tail feathers, very long and black, showing steel-blue and purple reflections, others brownish-black; bill black, long and curved: feet and tarsi black.

Length, 40 inches; wing 7.50; tail (including two central feathers) 28 inches; tarsus 2; bill 3.

Adult Female. — Above olive-brown; upper part of head reddish-brown; secondaries edged with rufus; cheeks, throat, and upper part of breast brownish-black; underpart pale, narrowly barred with black; tail brownish, with tinge of rufus; bill and feet as in the male, smaller.

The specimens above described are in my own collection.

EPIMACHUS ELLIOTI. *Ward.*

ELLIOT'S BIRD OF PARADISE.

Epimachus ellioti. — Ward, Proc. Zoöl. Soc., 1873, p. 748. — Elliot. Mon. Parad. pl. 20. — Beccari, Annali Mus. Civ. Genov. 7, p. 710. — Sharpe. Cat. Bds. Brit. Mus. 3, p. 163. — Gould, Bds. New Guinea, Pt. II.

HAB. — WAIGIOU.

All that is known regarding this beautiful bird may be summed up in very few words. A single specimen, supposed to have been obtained in New Guinea, came into the possession of Mr. Edwin Ward, by whom it was described. The type specimen has remained unique up to the present time, and is now in the British Museum. I append Mr. Elliot's description of the type specimen:—

"Top of the head rich amethyst; occiput and sides of neck also amethyst, changing in certain lights to a rich, light greenish gloss; back, wings, upper tail-coverts, and tail brilliant violet-purple; the wings and the tail also marbled with a dark amethyst hue like watered silk, changing according to the light; throat and upper portion of breast deep maroon color, with purple reflections; a narrow reddish-purple band crosses the lower part of the breast; sides of the breast, flanks, and rest of underparts dark green; the flank feathers much elongated, and stretching beyond the wings; beneath the shoulder of the wing spring two rows of plumes, which are greenish at the base, graduating into deep purple and terminating in a brilliant metallic blue, very much narrower in the upper row than the lower one. The plumage of the entire bird is very velvety in texture, and, with the exception of the metallic parts, appears black in ordinary lights; bill black, rich orange-yellow at the gape."

PLUVIANUS ÆGYPTIUS. (*Linn.*)

BLACK-HEADED PLOVER, OR CROCODILE BIRD.

Charadrius ægyptius. — Linn., Syst. Nat. 1, p. 254 (1776).
Le Pluvian. — Buff., Hist. Nat. Ois. 8, p. 104 (1781).
Green-headed Plover. — Lath., Gen. Syn. Suppl. 2, p. 320 (1787).
Charadrius melanocephalus. — Gmel., Syst. Nat. 1, p. 692.
Charadrius africanus. — Lath., Ind. Orn. Suppl., p. 67.
Pluvianus melanocephalus. — Vieill., Nouv. Dict. 27, p. 129.
Pluvianus chloroeephalus. — Vieill., tom. cit., p. 130.
Cusor charadroides. — Wagl., Syst. Av. Gen., sp. 6.
Ammoptila charadroides. — Swain's Class. Bds. 2, p. 364.
Cheilodromas melanocephalus. — Rupp., Mus. Senckenb. 2, p. 208.
Pluvianus ægyptius. — Strickl., Ann. & Mag. Nat. Hist. 10, p. 348.
Pluvianus ægyptiacus. — Brehm., Journ. für Orn., p. 102 (1853).
Hyas ægyptia. — Caban., Journ. für Orn., p. 71 (1854).
Cursorius ægyptius. — Schleg., Mus. Pays-Bas Cursores, p. 14 (1865).

THE Black-Headed Plover, or Crocodile Bird, as it is often called, is found commonly throughout Egypt and Nubia, in the vicinity of the Nile, wherever sand and mud banks are to be found. Specimens have been recorded from other parts of Africa, from Greece, the valley of the Jordan, and even from the coast of Spain; but Northeastern Africa must be considered as its true habitat, as it is there, and apparently there only, that it is abundant and resident throughout the year. There has been much controversy among naturalists as to whether this bird or the Spur-Winged Plover (*Hoplopterus spinosus*) should be considered the "Trochilus" spoken of by Herodotus, but any one who has seen both birds alive and investigated the matter cannot but give preference to the present species. During a trip up the Nile, I had the good fortune to procure a large series of specimens of both species; and while the Black-Headed Plover was invariably found upon the sand bars bordering the river banks, the Spur-Winged Plover kept to the fields, where we often observed it in large flocks.

Herodotus gives us the following account of the friendship which existed between this bird and the Crocodile: "All other birds and beasts avoid him, but he is at peace with the Trochilus because he receives benefit from that bird; for when the Crocodile gets out of the water on land, and then opens its jaws, which it does most commonly toward the west, the Trochilus enters its mouth and swallows the leeches. The Crocodile is so well pleased with this service that it never hurts the Trochilus." — *Herodotus, Euterpe*, 68.

Mr. F. H. Wenham says (Gould, Bds. of Asia, Pt. 17): "I may state that I believe the story of the Zic-Zac feeding in the Crocodile's mouth and picking his teeth to be a fable. I have seen upwards of a hundred Crocodiles, sometimes with this bird nestling under him, but never once in his jaws; and moreover, the fare obtained from the Crocodile's mouth would be exceedingly meagre; for, upon dissecting one of the several I must plead guilty to having shot, I could find nothing adhering to his palate, teeth, or jaws, — all were perfectly clean, as was the case also with regard to a still larger one, fourteen feet long, which I had an opportunity of examining; nor could I discover any of the leeches and other parasites said to exist there."

Cassell states, however (Bk. of Bds., Vol. IV. p. 11): "We can distinctly affirm that we have ourselves repeatedly *seen* the little creature performing the tooth-cleaning operation the ancients attributed to it, and which many modern writers have declared to be fabulous."

In the winter of 1874-75, I found it abundant on the Nile, between Essiout and Assouan, the banks of the river in that portion of the country being especially suited to its habits. We generally observed it running about on the sand banks, or making short flights from one point to another, seeming to be constantly in a state of activity.

According to Von Heuglin, the present species breeds in Egypt after the rainy season in Soudan. It makes no nest, simply depositing the eggs in a depression in the sand. The eggs are generally two in number. That the ancient Egyptians were acquainted with the bird is proved by the fact that it is frequently found occurring in the wall painting of the temples, and it is claimed that it is represented in the hieroglyphics by the sign U.

Adult Male.— Top and sides of the head, hind neck, back, and a band passing round and meeting on the breast, black; a band from the base of upper mandible passing around the crown to the nape, white; rump, white; most of the lesser wing coverts, scapulars, and upper tail coverts, bluish-gray; tail bluish-gray, tipped with white, with the exception of the central tail feathers showing a subterminal band of black; first primary having the outer web on the basal half white, rest of feather black; other primaries black on the basal half, then white, terminated with black; underparts white, washed with cream color and pale rufus on the abdomen and throat and under tail coverts; bill, blackish; iris, dark-brown; legs, bluish-gray.

Sexes similar.

Length, 8.50; wing, 5.50; tail, 2.60; tarsus, 1.35; bill, .95.

The figures represented in the plate are from specimens in my collection.

CHLAMYDODERA MACULATA. (*Gould.*)

SPOTTED BOWER-BIRD.

Calodera maculata. — Gould, Proc. Zoöl. Soc. (1836), p. 106, Synop. Birds Austr., pt. 1.
Chlamydera maculata. — Gould, Birds of Austr. (1837), pl. 1. — *Id.*, Birds Austr., Vol. IV., pl. 8. — G. R. Gray, Gen. Birds, Vol. II., p. 325.
Chlamydodera maculata. — Cab., Mus. Hein. Theil., I., p. 212. — Gould, Hand-B. Birds of Austr. (1865), Vol. I., p. 450. — Ramsay, Ibis (1866), p. 329. — Elliot, Monogr. Parad., pl. 30 (1873).

HABITAT. — NEW SOUTH WALES, EASTERN AUSTRALIA.

THE present species represents a very curious family of birds, closely allied to the Birds of Paradise. Mr. Gould, who discovered the species, gives the best account of it that I have been able to find. I therefore quote his observations concerning it: "I observed this bird to be tolerably abundant at Brezi, on the river Mokai, to the northward of the Liverpool Plains; it is also equally numerous in all the low scrubby ranges in the neighborhood of the Namoi, as well as in the open brushes which intersect the plains on its borders, and collections from Moreton Bay generally contain examples. Still, from the extreme shyness of its disposition, the bird is seldom seen by ordinary travellers, and it must be under very peculiar circumstances that it can be approached sufficiently close to observe its colors. The Spotted Bower-Bird has a harsh, grating, scolding note, which is generally uttered when its haunts are intruded on, and by which its presence is detected when it would otherwise escape observation. When disturbed it takes to the topmost branches of the loftiest trees, and frequently flies off to another neighborhood. In many of its actions, and in the greater part of its economy, much similarity exists between this species and the Satin Bower-Bird, particularly in the curious habit of constructing an artificial bower or playing-place. I was so far fortunate as to discover several of these bowers during my journey in the interior, the finest of which I succeeded in bringing to England; it is now in the British Museum. The situations of these runs or bowers are much varied; I found them both on the plains studded with Myalls (*Acacia pendula*) and other small trees, and in the brushes clothing the lower hills. They are considerably longer and more avenue-like than those of the Satin Bower-Bird, being in many instances three feet in length. They are outwardly built of twigs, and beautifully lined with tall grasses, so disposed that their heads nearly meet : the decorations are very profuse, and consist of bivalve shells, crania of small mammalia and other bones bleached by exposure to the rays of the sun or from the camp-fires of the natives. Evident indications of high instinct appear throughout the whole of the bower and decorations formed by this species, particularly in the manner in which the stones are placed within the bower, apparently to keep the grasses with which it is lined fixed firmly in their places; these stones diverge from the mouth of the run on each side so as to form little paths, while the immense collection of decorative materials are placed in a heap before the entrance of the avenue, — the arrangement being the same at both ends. In some of the larger bowers, which had evidently been resorted to for many years, I have seen half a bushel of bones, shells, etc., at each of the entrances. I frequently found these structures at a considerable distance from the rivers, from the borders of which they could alone have procured the shells and small round pebbly stones; their collection and transportation must therefore be a task of great labor. I fully ascertained that these runs, like those of the Satin Bower-Bird, formed the rendezvous of many individuals; for, after secreting myself for a short space of time, near one of them, I killed two males which I had previously seen running through the avenue. The natives unhesitatingly state that the bird makes its nest in the high gum-trees; and Mr. Charles Coxen, of Brisbane, found a nest of the *Chlamydodera maculata* with young birds in it some years ago on Oaky Creek, near the present Jondary, a head station on the Darling Downs; the nest was built in one of the Myrtaceæ overhanging a water-hole, near a scrub on which a tower was built, and was in form very similar to that of the Common Thrush of Europe, being of a cup shape, constructed of dried sticks, with a slight lining of feathers and fine grass. The eggs are still unknown."

Having only one poor specimen of the species, I give Mr. Gould's description of it in full : —

Male. — "Crown of the head, ear coverts, and throat rich brown, each feather being surrounded by a narrow line of black ; feathers on the crown small and tipped with silvery gray ; a beautiful band of elongated feathers of a light rose-pink crosses the back of the neck, forming a broad fan-like occipital crest. All the upper surface wings and tail of a deep brown, every feather of the back, rump, scapularies and secondaries tipped with a large round spot of rich buff; primaries slightly tipped with white. All the tail feathers terminated with buffy-white, under surface grayish-white ; feathers of the flanks marked with faint transverse zigzag lines of light brown."

The female lacks the rose-colored patch on the nape, otherwise resembling the male.

LOPHORINA ATRA. (*Bodd.*)

SUPERB BIRD OF PARADISE.

L'oiseau de Paradis de la Nouvelle Guinée dit le Superbe. — Brisson, Orn., III., p. 169 (1760). — D'Aubent, Planches
    Enluminées, III., pl. 632 (1774).
Oiseau de Paradis à gorge violette. — Sonn., Voy. Nouv. Guinée, p. 157, pl. 96 (1776).
Paradisea superba. — Pennant. in Forster, Ind. Zool., p. 40 (1781). — Scopoli, Del. Faun. et Flor. Insubr., II., p. 88
    (1783). — Shaw, Gen. Zoöl., VII., p. 494, pls. 63-65 (1809). — Id. & Nodder, Nat. Misc., XXIV., pl. 1021
    (1813). — Wagler, Syst. Av. Paradisen, sp. 5 (1827). — Wallace, Ibis, 1859, p. 111.
Superb Bird of Paradise. — Lath., Gen. Syn. Vol. I., part 2, p. 479 (1782).
Paradisea atra. — Bodd., Tabl. Pl. Enl., D'Aubent, p. 38 (1783).
Le superbe. — Vieill., Ois. Dor., II., pl. 7 (1802). — Levaill, Hist. Nat. Ois. Parad. I., pls. 14, 15 (1806).
Paradisea furcata. — Bechst., Kurze. Uebers, p. 132 (1811).
Lophorina superba. — Vieill., N. Dict. d'Hist Nat., XVIII., p. 184 (1817). — Id., Gal. Ois., I., p. 149, pl. 98 (1825). —
    Less. Traité, p 337 (1831). — Id., Ois. Parad. Syn., p. 12 (1835). — Id., Hist. Nat. Ois. Parad., pls. 13,14 (1835). —
    Bonap., Consp. Gen. Av., p. 414 (1850). — Wall., Ibis, 1861. p. 287. — Salvad., Ann. Mus. Civic. Genov., IX.,
    p. 190 (1876). — Sharpe, Cat. Bds, III., p. 179 (1877). — Gould, Bds. New Guinea, pt. 6 (1878).
Epimachus ater. — Schl., Mus. Pays-Bas, Coraces, p. 96. note (1867).
Lophorina atra. — Wallace, Malay Arch., II., p. 249 (1869). — Elliot, Monogr. Parad., pl. 11 (1873). — Salvad., Ann.
    Mus. Civic. Genov., VII., p. 783 (1875). — Beccari, tom. cit., p. 712 (1875). — Sclater, Ibis, 1876, p. 251.

HABITAT. — NEW GUINEA.

THE beautiful and curious species which forms the subject of the present article is a native of Northern New Guinea, where it appears to be rather uncommon. Very few specimens have as yet reached this country, and none of the naturalists who have visited New Guinea have given us an account of its habits. Dr. Beccari mentions it, but merely says: "Lophorina atra is rather rarer than Parotia, but I must tell you that the abundance of fruit-eating birds in a given locality depends principally on the season at which certain kinds of fruit are ripe, therefore a species may be common in a place one month and become rare or completely disappear in the next, when the season of the fruit on which it lives has passed."

Adult Male. — General plumage very dark brown, almost black, showing bronze and purple reflections in some lights. Top of head and large triangular shield extending from the lower part of the throat rich metallic green, showing light purple in some lights and steely blue in others. A broad, elevated mantle or shield of velvety black plumes, with bronze reflections. A small double crest of purplish-black feathers at the base of the upper mandible; bill and feet black.

Length, 9; wing. 5; tail, 3.4; tarsus, 1.20; bill, 1.

Adult Female. — Above chocolate brown; top and sides of the head dark brown; white spotted feathers over the eye. Wing coverts and quills dark brown, showing reddish on the edges. Tail brown. Throat whitish, the feathers being black, tipped with white. Under parts buff-white, showing rufous tinge on flanks and under tail coverts, the whole barred with dull brown. Wing coverts rufous, barred with brown.

The specimens figured in the plate are in my own collection.

PARADISEA SANGUINEA. *Shaw.*

RED BIRD OF PARADISE.

Paradisea sanguinea. — Shaw, Gen. Zoöl. (1809), Vol. VII., pt. 1, pl. 39, p. 487. — Elliot, Mon. Parad., pl. 5 (1873). — Gould, Bds. New Guinea, pt. 4 (1877).
Paradisea rubra. — Vieill., Gal. Ois. (1825), Vol. I., p. 152, pl. 99. — Wall., Proc. Zoöl. Soc. (1862), p. 160. — *Id.*, Ibis (1859), p. 111; (1861), p. 287. — Malay Arch., Vol. II., pp. 215, 221, 243.
Red Bird of Paradise. — Lath., Gen. Hist. of Birds (1822). Vol. III., p. 186.
L'Oiseau de Paradis Rouge. — Levaill., Hist. Nat. des Ois. Parad., Vol. I., pl. 6 (1806).
Le Paradis Rouge. — Vieill., Ois. d'Or., Vol. II., pl. 14, pl. 3 (1802).

HABITAT. — WAIGIOU, GUEMIEN, AND BATANA.

VERY little is known regarding this beautiful species, although specimens are not uncommon in collections, and I must again quote Mr. Wallace, who has done so much to make us acquainted with birds of this family, in regard to its capture. He says: "When I first arrived I was surprised at being told that there were no Paradise birds at Muka, although there were plenty at Bessir, a place where the natives caught them and prepared the skins. I assured the people I had heard the cry of these birds close to the village; but they would not believe that I could know their cry. However, the very first time I went into the forest I not only heard but saw them, and was convinced there were plenty about; but they were very shy, and it was some time before we got any. My hunter first shot a female, and I one day got very close to a fine male. He was, as I expected, the rare red species, *Paradisea rubra*, which alone inhabits this island and is found nowhere else. He was quite low down, running along a bough, searching for insects, almost like a Woodpecker; and the long black riband-like filaments in his tail hung down in the most graceful double curve imaginable. I covered him with my gun, and was going to use the barrel which had a very small charge of powder and No. 8 shot, so as not to injure his plumage; but the gun missed fire, and he was off in an instant among the thickest jungle. Another day we saw no less than eight fine males at different times, and fired four times at them; but though other birds at the same distance almost always dropped, these all got away, and I began to think we were never to get this magnificent species. At length the fruit ripened on the fig-tree close to my house, and many birds came to feed on it; and one morning, as I was taking my coffee, a male Paradise bird was seen to settle on its top. I seized my gun, ran under the tree, and, gazing up, could see it flying across from branch to branch, seizing a fruit here and another there; and then, before I could get a sufficient aim to shoot at such a height (for it was one of the loftiest trees of the tropics), it was away into the forest. They now visited the tree every morning, but they stayed so short a time, their motions were so rapid, and it was so difficult to see them, owing to the lower trees which impeded the view, that it was only after several days' watching, and one or two misses, that I brought down my bird, — a male in the most magnificent plumage. . . . I had only shot two Paradiseas on my tree when they ceased visiting it, either owing to the fruit becoming scarce or that they were wise enough to know there was danger. We continued to hear and see them in the forest, but after a month had not succeeded in shooting any more; and as my chief object in visiting Waigiou was to get these birds, I determined to go to Bessir, where there are a number of Papuans who catch and preserve them. I hired a small outrigger boat for this journey, and left one of my men to guard my house and goods. . . . My first business was to send for the men who were accustomed to catch the Birds of Paradise. Several came, and I showed them my hatchets, beads, knives, and handkerchiefs, and explained to them as well as I could by signs the price I would give for fresh-killed specimens. It is the universal custom to pay for everything in advance, but only one man ventured to take goods to the value of two birds. The rest were suspicious, and wanted to see the result of the first bargain with the strange white man, the only one who had ever come to their island. After three days my man brought me the first bird, — a very fine specimen, and alive, but tied up in a small bag, and consequently its tail and wing feathers were very much crushed and injured. I tried to explain to him, and to others that came with him, that I wanted them as perfect as possible, and that they should either kill them or keep them on a perch with a string to their leg. As they were now apparently satisfied that all was fair, and that I had no ulterior designs upon them, six others took away goods, some for one bird, some for more, and one for as many as six. They said they had to go a long way for them, and that they would come back as soon as they caught any. At intervals of a few days or a week some of them would return, bringing me one or more birds; but, though they did not bring any more in bags, there was not much improvement in their condition. As they caught them a long way off in the forest, they would scarcely ever come with one, but would tie it by the legs to a stick, and put it in their house till they caught another. The poor creature would make violent efforts to escape, would get among the ashes, or hang suspended by the leg till the limb was swollen or half putrefied, and sometimes died of starvation and worry. One had its beautiful head all defiled by pitch from a dammar torch; another had been so long dead that its stomach was turning green. Luckily, however, the skin and plumage of these birds are so firm and strong that they bear washing and cleaning better than almost any other sort; and I was generally able to clean them so well that they did not perceptibly differ from those I had shot myself. Some few were brought me the same day they were caught, and I had an opportunity of examining them in all their beauty and vivacity. As soon as I found they were generally brought alive, I set one of my men to make a large bamboo cage, with troughs for food and water, hoping to be able to keep some of them. I got the natives to bring me branches of a fruit they were very fond of; and I was pleased to find they ate it greedily and would also take any number of live grasshoppers I gave them, stripping off the legs and wings, and then swallowing them. They drank plenty of water, and were in constant motion, jumping about the cage from perch to perch, clinging to the top and sides, and rarely resting a moment the first day till nightfall. The second day they were always less active, although they would eat as freely as before; and on the morning of the third day they were almost always found dead at the bottom of the cage, without any apparent cause. Some of them ate boiled rice, as well as fruits and insects; but, after trying many in succession, not one out of ten lived more than three days. The second or third day they would be dull, and in several cases they were seized with convulsions and fell off the perch, dying a few hours afterwards. I tried immature as well as full-plumaged birds, but with no better success, and at length gave it up as a hopeless task, and confined my attention to preserving specimens in as good a condition as possible. The Red Birds of Paradise are not shot with blunt arrows, as in the Aru Islands and some parts of New Guinea, but are snared in a very ingenious manner. A large climbing Arum bears a red reticulated fruit, of which the birds are very fond. The hunters fasten this fruit on a stout forked stick, and provide themselves with a fine but strong cord. They then seek out some tree in the forest on which these birds are accustomed to perch, and, climbing up it, fasten the stick to a branch, and arrange the cord in a noose so ingeniously that, when the bird comes to eat the fruit, its legs are caught; and by pulling the end of the cord which hangs down to the ground, it comes free from the branch and brings down the bird. Sometimes, when food is abundant elsewhere, the hunter sits from morning till night under his tree, with the cord in his hand, and even for two or three whole days in succession, without even getting a bite; while, on the other hand, if very lucky, he may get two or three birds in a day."

Adult Male. — Front of head, cheeks, and throat rich metallic green; feathers elevated over the eyes. Base of head upper part of back, breast, and rump orange-yellow. Wings, back, underparts, and tail dark chestnut-brown. Long flowing plumes spring from under the wings, deep red at the base, but gradually whitening to the tips. Two long black shafts extend from the lower part of the back and fall in long graceful curves. These are entirely webless in adult, but are webbed at the tips in the young bird, in which state the shafts are brownish and the webs pale brown.

Length, 13.50; wing, 7; tail, 5.50; bill, 1; tarsus, 1.80; long shafts in adult specimen above described, 22 inches.

Adult Female. — Front of head, cheeks, and throat chestnut-brown; upper breast and base of head yellowish, shading into brownish-yellow on back. Rest of plumage chestnut-brown. Feet and tarsus black; bill brown color.

The specimens above described are in my collection.

PARADISEA APODA. *Linn.*

THE GREATER BIRD OF PARADISE

The Greater Bird of Paradise. — Edwards, Bds., III., pl. 110.
L'Oiseau de Paradis. — Brisson, Orn., II., pl. 13, p. 130.
Paradisea apoda. — Linn, Syst. Nat., I., p. 166; Wagler, Syst. Avis Paradisea. sp. 1; Bonap. Consp. Gen. Av., I., p. 412; Gray, P. Z. S. (1861), p. 436; Wallace, Ibis (1859), p. 111 (1861), p. 289; Schleg. Mus. Pays-Bas. Coraces, p. 78; Wallace, Malay Archip., II., p. 238; Gray, Hand-b. Bds., II., p. 16; Elliot, Monograph Paradisidæ, pl. 1; Salvad. Ann. Mus. Civ. Genor., IX., p. 191; Sharpe, Cat. Bds., III., p. 167; Gould, Bds. New Guinea, pt. IX.
Paradisea major. — Shaw, Gen. Zoöl., VII., p. 480, pl. 58; Less., Ois. de Parad. Synop., p. 6; *Id.*, Hist. Nat. p. 155, pl. 6.
Paradisea apods. var. Wallaciana. — Gray, P. Z. S. (1858), p. 181.

HABITAT. — ARRU ISLANDS AND S. E. NEW GUINEA.

M̲R. GOULD, in his "Birds of New Guinea," gives a condensed history of the present species, quoting from other authors. It is so well chosen that I give it entire: "'When the earliest European voyagers,' writes Mr. Wallace, in his 'Malay Archipelago,' 'reached the Moluccas in search of cloves and nutmegs, which were then rare and precious spices, they were presented with the dried skins of birds so strange and beautiful as to excite the admiration even of those wealth-seeking rovers. The Malay traders gave them the name of "Manukdewata" (or God's Birds), and the Portuguese, finding that they had no feet or wings, and not being able to learn anything authentic about them, called them "Passaros de Sol" (or Birds of the Sun); while the learned Dutchmen, who wrote in Latin, called them "Avis paradiseus" (or Paradise Bird). John van Linschoten gives these names in 1598, and tells us that no one has seen these birds alive, for they live in the air, always turning towards the sun, and never lighting on the earth till they die; for they have neither feet nor wings, as, he adds, may be seen by the birds carried to India, and sometimes to Holland: but being very costly they are rarely seen in Europe. More than one hundred years later Mr. William Funnel, who accompanied Dampier, and wrote an account of the voyage, saw specimens at Amboyna, and was told that they came to Banda to eat nutmegs, which intoxicated them and made them fall down senseless, when they were killed by ants. Down to 1760, when Linnæus named the largest species Paradisea apoda (the Footless Paradise Bird), no perfect specimen had been seen in Europe, and absolutely nothing was known about them. And even now, a hundred years later, most books state that they migrate annually to Ternate, Banda, and Amboyna, whereas the fact is that they are as completely unknown in these islands in a wild state as they are in England.' I may remark that Edwards had probably a complete specimen in 1750, as he mentions the figures in the older authors, such as Willoughby, and remarks, 'As none of these were satisfactory to me, I have given this figure and description of a *perfect bird*, which may more than answer the purposes of so many.' And again, 'It hath legs and feet of a moderate proportion and strength for its bigness, shaped much like those of Pyes or Jays, of a dark brown color, armed with claws of middling strength.' The fact remains, however, that the vast majority of skins received in Europe before Mr. Wallace's expedition were mutilated and footless. He writes, 'The native mode of preserving them is to cut off the wings and feet, and then skin the body up to the beak, taking out the skulls. A stout stick is then run up through the specimen, coming out at the mouth. Round this some leaves are stuffed, and the whole is wrapped up in a palm-spathe and dried in the smoky hut. By this plan the head, which is really large, is shrunk up almost to nothing, the body is much reduced and shortened, and the greatest prominence is given to the flowing plumage. Some of these native skins are very clean, and often have wings and feet left on; others are dreadfully stained with smoke, and all give a most erroneous idea of the proportions of the living bird.' The following notes on the habits are also given by Mr. Wallace: 'The Great Bird of Paradise is very active and vigorous, and seems to be in constant motion all day long. It is very abundant, small flocks of females and young males being constantly met with'; and though the full-plumaged birds are less plentiful, their loud cries, which are heard daily, show that they also are very numerous. Their note is "Wawk-wawkwauk-wok-wok-wok," and is so loud and shrill as to be heard a great distance, and to form the most prominent and characteristic animal sound in the Arru Islands. The mode of nidification is unknown, but the natives told me that the nest was made of leaves placed on an ants' nest, or on some projecting limb of a very lofty tree, and believe that it contains only one young bird. The egg is quite unknown, and the natives declared they had never seen it; and a very high reward offered for one by a Dutch official did not meet with success. They moult about January or February, and in May, when they are in full plumage, the males assemble early in the morning to exhibit themselves. This habit enables the natives to obtain specimens with comparative ease. As soon as they find that the birds have fixed upon a tree on which to assemble, they build a little shelter of palm-leaves in a convenient place among the branches; and the hunter ensconces himself in it before daylight, armed with his bow and a number of arrows terminating in a round knob. A boy waits at the foot of the tree, and when the birds come at sunrise, and a sufficient number have assembled, and have begun to dance, the hunter shoots with his blunt arrow so strongly as to stun the bird, which drops down, and is secured and killed by the boy without its plumage being injured by a drop of blood. The rest take no notice, and fall one after another till some of them take the alarm.' The Paradisea apoda, as far as we have any certain knowledge, is confined to the mainland of the Arru Islands, never being found in the smaller islands which surround the centre mass. It is certainly not found in any of the parts of New Guinea visited by the Malay and Bugis traders, nor in any of the other islands where Birds of Paradise are obtained. But this is by no means conclusive evidence, for it is only in certain localities that the natives prepare skins, and in other places the same birds may be abundant without ever becoming known. It is, therefore, quite possible that this species may inhabit the great southern mass of New Guinea, from which Arru has been separated; while its near ally (P. papuana) is confined to the northwestern peninsula. I may remark that Mr. Wallace's prediction that this species would be found on the southern part of New Guinea has been verified by Signor D'Albertis, who recently showed me a fine skin obtained by himself on the Fly River, far in the interior of southwestern New Guinea. This specimen was a trifle smaller and brighter in color than Mr. Wallace's Arru specimens, of which I have a fine series."

The specimens are in my own collection. I consider a detailed description of the present species unnecessary, the plate being exceedingly accurate.

IBIS RELIGIOSA.

IBIS ÆTHIOPICA. (*Lath.*)

SACRED IBIS.

Tantalus æthiopicus. — Lath. Ind. Orn. (1790), Vol. II., p. 706, sp. 12.
Numenius ibis. — Cuv. Ann. du Mus. (1805), Vol. IV., p. 116, t. 53.
Ibis religiosa. — Savig. Hist. de l'Egypte (1810), Ois. t. 7, fig. 1 (text), Vol. III., p. 392 ; Vieill. Nouv. Dict. Hist. Nat.
    (1817), Vol. XVI., p. 9 ; Temm. Man. Ornith. (1820), Vol. IV., p. 390 ; Vieill. Ency. Meth. (1823),
    p. 1144 ; Wagl. Syst. Av. (1827), sp. 2 ; Hemp. & Ehrenb. Sym. Phys. (1828), p. 17 ; Cuv. Regn. Anim.
    (1829), p. 519 ; Less. Trait. Orn. (1831), p. 568, sp. 15 ; Wagl. Isis (1832), p. 1231 ; Sykes, Proc.
    Zoöl. Soc. (1832), p. 160, sp. 188 ; Bon. Consp. Gen. Av. (1857), Vol. II., p. 151 ; Schleg. Mus.
    Pays-B. (1863), Livr. IV., p. 12 ; Kirk, Ibis (1864), p. 364 ; Bree, B. Eur., 1st ed., Vol. IV., p. 45,
    pl. 13 ; Schleg. Proc. Zoöl. Soc. (1866), p. 425 ; Sharpe, Proc. Zoöl. Soc. (1871). p. 614.
Ibis egretta. — Temm. Man. Orn., Vol. IV., p. 391 ; Bon. Consp. Gen. Av. (1857), Vol. II., p. 151.
Ibis molusca. — Cuv. MS. Mus. Paris ; *Id.*, Regn. Anim., p. 320 ; Less. Trait. Orn. (1831), p. 568, sp. 13.
Tantalus ibis. — J. Brookes, Linn. Trans, Vol. XVI. (1830), p. 499.
Ibis strictipennis. — Gould, Proc. Zoöl. Soc. (1837). p. 106 ; Bon. Consp. Gen. Av. (1857), Vol. II., p. 151 ; Schleg. Mus.
    Pays-B. (1863), Livr. IV., p. 14 ; Garrod, Proc. Zoöl. Soc. (1873), pp. 467, 638.
Threskiornis strictipennis. — Gould, B. Austr., Vol. VI., pl. 46 ; *Id.*, Hand-b. B. Austr. (1865), Vol. II., p. 284.
Threskiornis æthiopicus. — Gray, App. List. Gen. Birds (1842), p. 13 ; Gurney, Ibis (1860), p. 219, (1865), p. 275.
Geronticus strictipennis. — Gray, Gen. B. (1849), Vol. III., p. 567, sp. 7 ; *Id.*, Hand-b. B. (1871), pl. 3, p. 40.
Geronticus æthiopicus. — Gray. Gen. B. (1849), Vol. III., p. 566, sp. 5 ; Layard, B. S. Afr. (1867), p. 320, sp. 604 ; Gray,
    Hand-b. B. (1871). pt. 3, p. 40 ; Bartlett, Ibis (1876), p. 211.
Ibis æthiopica. — Von Heugl. Syst. Ueber. Vog Nordost.-Afr. (1855), p. 213, sp. 633 ; Gurney, Ibis (1868), p. 259 ; Finsch.
    & Hartl. Vog. Ost. Afr. (1870), p. 783 ; Gurney, Anderss. B. Damaral. (1872), p. 297 ; Shelley, B.
    Egypt. (1872), p. 261 ; Heugl. Ornith. Nordost.-Afr. (1873), Band II., Abth. 1., p. 1135 : Ayres, Ibis
    (1874), p. 105 ; Elliot, Proc. Zoöl. Soc. (1877). p. 486.
Thresciornis religiosa. — Hartl. Syst. Orn. W. Afr. (1857), p. 1232, sp. 658 ; Gurney, Ibis (1859), p. 153, sp. 9 (1865), p. 275.

THERE is, in all probability, no other bird which by name is as familiar to the educated world at large as the Sacred Ibis. It has an interest for the antiquarian as well as the naturalist, and is associated with Egypt, its mummies and its temples. It is no longer found in Egypt proper, although it was very abundant there in ancient times, and was worshipped by the ancient Egyptians. Upon its death it was carefully embalmed, and great quantities of mummies of these birds are found in the tombs and pits throughout Egypt. Strabo states that every street in Alexandria was full of them in his time, and they were very useful in picking up all kinds of offal thrown out of the shops. They were very troublesome and dirty, and were prevented with difficulty from polluting what was clean and not intended for them. It was the emblem of Troth, the scribe of Osiris, and its portrait is still to be seen on many of the monuments and temples. It is known to the natives by the name of "Abu Kedun" (Father of the Bills), and at the present time seldom ranges farther than 15° north. It generally arrives at Kartoum about the last of July and remains there to breed, but it is much more abundant a few degrees farther south, in the neighborhood of the White Nile. Its food consists principally of fishes and aquatic insects, and it is claimed that it destroys and eats snakes. It is said that Cuvier discovered the remains of a snake in the body of a mummied Ibis.

Adult Male. — Head and neck naked, skin black ; primaries tipped with greenish black. Tertials much lengthened, falling over and covering the lower part of the wing ; they are dark purple in the adult. Rest of plumage white. Legs, horn color ; bill, black ; iris, red-brown.

The young bird has the neck covered with short white feathers.

Length, 30 ; wing, 14 ; tail, 6 ; bill, 7 ; tarsus, 3.75.

DREPANORNIS ALBERTISI. *Sclater.*

D'ALBERTIS' BIRD OF PARADISE

Drepanornis Albertisi. — Sclater, P. Z. S. (1873), p. 558, p. 47. — Elliot, Monograph, Paradiseidæ, pl. 21. — Gould, Bds.
New Guinea, pt. 1.
Epimachus Wilhelminæ. — Meyer, J. F. O. (1873), p. 404. — *Id.,* Ibis (1874), p. 303.

HABITAT. — NEW GUINEA.

THIS wonderful bird is one of the rarest of its family. At first sight it appears dull in plumage, but a close exam-
ination reveals such exquisite shadings of gold, bronze, and purple as to entitle it to rank as beautiful as well as curious.
It was first discovered by Signor d'Albertis during his explorations in the island of New Guinea. He obtained it at Mount
Arfak. In writing of this species, he says: "This will probably prove to be a new bird, both generically and specifically.
It is a very rare bird, and many of the natives did not know it; but others called it 'Quarna.' The peculiarity of this
species consists in the formation of the bill, head, and softness of the plumage. At first it does not appear to have the
beauty peculiar to other birds of this class; but when observed more closely, in a strong light, the plumage is seen to be
rich and brilliant; the feathers rising from the base of the beak are of a metallic green and reddish copper-color; the
feathers of the breast, when smooth, are of a violet-gray, and when raised form a semicircle round the body, reflecting a
rich golden color; other violet-gray feathers arise from the flanks, which are edged by a rich metallic violet tint, and when
the plumage is entirely expanded the bird appears as if it had formed two semicircles round itself, and is very handsome.
The tail and wing feathers are yellowish; underneath they are of a darker shade. The head is barely covered with small
round feathers, which are rather deficient at the back of the ear. The shoulders are tobacco-color, and under the throat
black, blending into olive. The breast is violet-gray, banded by a line of olive, the rest white. The beak is black, eyes
chestnut, and the feet of a dark leaden color. This species is met with in the vicinity of Mount Arfak. Its food is not
known, nothing having been found in the stomachs of those prepared except clean water."

The following careful descriptions are taken from Mr. Elliot's Monograph of the Paradiseidæ : —

"*Male.* — Head covered with short, rather stiff light-brown feathers, tipped with deep purple. Two spots of
metallic-blue feathers between the eyes and bill, projecting above the eyes like horns ; a spot of bare skin behind the eyes,
apparently red. Neck and back rufous-brown. Primaries blackish-brown, edged with light rufous feathers on the outer
webs. Secondaries light rufous-brown on outer web, black on the inner, edged with very light reddish-brown. The three
innermost secondaries light reddish-brown on both webs. Upper tail coverts and tail bright reddish-brown. Chin and
throat metallic deep purple, black in certain lights. Breast covered with long feathers, gray, with rich purple reflections,
and edged on the lower part with dull green, crossing the body in a narrow bar. From either side, near the shoulder of
the wing, spring two tufts of feathers that extend beyond the breast-shield, of an intense metallic fiery red, tipped with
purple. These, when not elevated, are altogether hidden by the outer feathers, which are uniform purple like the breast.
From the flanks, just above the termination of the breast-shields, on either side project two long tufts of plumes, which
extend to the end of the tail coverts, of the same color as the breast, brownish-gray, each feather tipped with very brilliant

deep purple. The abdomen and under tail coverts pure white, the former streaked with purplish-gray on the upper portion. Bill very long, slender, and much curved, black. Feet and tarsi dull lead color.

"*Female.* — Head chestnut-brown. Back and wings rufous-brown. Primaries and secondaries blackish-brown on inner web, outer web brown. Upper tail coverts and tail light red. Chin and throat blackish-brown, each feather with a central streak of light brown. Breast light brown, irregularly barred with dark brown. Flanks and lower parts of body yellowish-brown, indistinctly barred with dark brown, except in the centre of abdomen, which is light reddish-white. Thighs reddish, barred with brown. Under tail coverts pale reddish. Iris chestnut. Bill long, curved, and slender like that of the male, black. Feet and tarsi lead color."

www.ingramcontent.com/pod-product-compliance
Lightning Source LLC
Chambersburg PA
CBHW022337020726
47500CB00004B/1161